Cyclops and
the Greenbeans

Sam McBratney

Illustrated by Terry McKenna

Sydney Greenbean went down to the shops to buy some jelly babies. These were his favourite sweets at the moment. Sometimes he ate their heads first and sometimes he ate them whole.

Robert Foote came too. He lived next door and the two boys were usually good friends. It was Robert who first noticed the bike behind them. "Hey, Syd, look at your bike. It's following us."

Sydney saw that this was true. No one was wheeling his bike and no one was riding it, yet it travelled along the middle of the pavement with its pedals slowly turning of their own accord.

The bicycle's name was Cyclops. It had a name because Sydney Greenbean believed in giving names to all his belongings. This had been his policy since he was four.

Cyclops looked like any other one-year-old bicycle that had been knocked about a bit. His front mudguard had a permanent twist since that nasty collision with the gate-post, and his transfers had faded away like old tattoos. His gears sometimes slipped, his rims were rusty, his bell whined instead of ringing clearly and he needed new brake blocks. No one would have suspected that here was a bicycle with rare abilities and a strange future.

They had almost reached the shops.

"Well, I think I'll buy my jelly babies anyway," Sydney said, "and see if he follows us home again."

It did.

Mr and Mrs Greenbean happened to be upstairs when Sydney came back from the shops. They were talking loudly about decorating, so it was not easy for their son to get a word in edgeways. "Hey, Dad, Cyclops followed me down to the shops."

"Jolly good," Mr Greenbean said, accepting a jelly baby, "but I thought we had decided on yellow, Margaret. It has to be yellow."

"I don't see why it has to be yellow."

"Because yellow is fresh and crisp and it catches the early morning sunshine."

"You sound like a cornflake, Wilfred," said Mrs Greenbean, staring at the door.

The bicycle was there, right behind
Sydney.

"What is that thing doing up the
stairs?" asked Mrs Greenbean.

"That's what I was telling you,"
Sydney said. "It follows me. Watch this."

As Sydney walked round the carpet in a
neat circle, Cyclops wheeled round the
carpet in the same neat circle.

"Glory be!" said Mrs Greenbean.

"Fancy that!" said Mr Greenbean. "I've
seen everything now. Let us go downstairs
and talk this over calmly. Something will
have to be done about this!"

The sign above the door in the High Street said:

CROSSROADS
BICYCLE SHOP

Mr Greenbean, Sydney and Cyclops passed under the sign, in that order, and entered the shop. Mr Greenbean was nervous because he could not quite make up his mind what he ought to say. Fortunately the shop was empty, except for the man who appeared behind the counter with an oily rag in his hands. "And what can I do for you, Sir?"

"Some time ago you sold us this bicycle which you see before you," Mr Greenbean began. "Perhaps you remember us. It was the month of March."

"I sell a lot o' bikes in March, Sir. Spring time, you see."

"Well, the fact is that there's something wrong with it. Show the man what we mean, Sydney."

Sydney obliged. He and Cyclops performed a figure-of-eight around the shop floor, one after the other.

"Do you see what I'm getting at?" said Mr Greenbean. "That just isn't normal."

The shop man scratched his face with an oily finger, and left an oily mark there. "I've been in this business forty-odd years," he said, "and I ain't never seen anything like it. And that's a fact."

All the same, he examined the bicycle for a quarter of an hour, free of charge.

"This here bike is in right good working order, Sir. Normal wear and tear, of course, but as far as that other business about following people is concerned … there ain't nothing I can do. I can only think it's got to do with these fancy computers they got nowadays."

Mr Greenbean thanked him for his opinion. When he and Sydney and Cyclops got home again, Mrs Greenbean declared that she was not satisfied. "If there is nothing wrong with that bike," she said, "then it must be our Sydney."

"There's nothing wrong with me," said Sydney.

"Then why does it follow *you* around? Why not someone else? Why doesn't it follow Robert Foote, for goodness sake? Have you suddenly turned magnetic?"

There was no answer to these questions, so they sent for Dr McCackerel. He came at once because, he said, this sounded like a most interesting case. Dr McCackerel agreed with Sydney. "Fit as a fiddle! Not a thing wrong with him. Live to be a hundred, I shouldn't wonder."

Mr Greenbean said he was relieved to hear it. "But Dr McCackerel, have you no

idea what is happening? I mean to say, if bicycles start to move of their own accord ... well, whatever next?"

The doctor patted Sydney's dad on the shoulder. "Gently does it, old Bean. Life is strange and rich and exciting, after all—and this is one of those strange and rich and exciting things. Let me know if there are any developments."

Away he went, whistling. The Greenbeans felt much better after his visit. Sydney soon found that having Cyclops around could be useful. Every now and then, he and some of his friends played football with Danny Viking and some of his friends. These games of football were not arranged by anyone—they just seemed to happen. And when they happened, Sydney Greenbean liked to win.

So did Danny Viking.

One of these games took place on Saturday morning. By half-time, things looked black indeed for the Greenbean team. They were down by eight goals to five. This was because Sydney's men were a man short. Their regular goalie had chicken pox.

"We're too good for you," said Danny Viking, who was celebrating already. "Admit it. We've got you whipped."

In sheer desperation, Sydney stuck Cyclops in the Greenbean goalmouth and told him to stay there.

The second half began where the first had left off—with the ball at Danny Viking's feet. Down the wing he flew, brushing aside Robert Foote's tackle with scornful ease. Now he cut inside and prepared to thump the ball through the goals to make it nine–five.

A bicycle reared up in front of him and
smashed the ball upfield with its front
wheel. Robert Foote collected the rebound,
lobbed it to Sydney, who scored a beauty
with his head.

It was the first of many. The Greenbeans
won nineteen–eleven.

"CHEATERS!" raged Danny Viking.
"You're nothing but a bunch of cheaters."
With these words he stomped off the pitch
as if he would never play football again.
Even his own team were disgusted to see
what a bad loser he was.

The Greenbeans gathered round Cyclops to praise his goalkeeping, and then went home for something to eat.

At half-past twelve that same day, the phone rang in Mrs Greenbean's hall. She answered it, and listened for a while. Then she put a hand over the receiver and spoke to her husband. "Wilfred, it's that man, Harry Viking, on the line—the one who works for *The Star*."

Mr Greenbean thoughtfully lowered his crossword. "What does he want, dear?"

"He says he's heard about Sydney's bike—wants to know if he can talk to him about it and maybe get a picture or two for the paper."

Mr Greenbean turned to Sydney, who was listening with interest. "You don't mind being in the papers, do you, son?"

"I *want* to be in the papers," said Sydney.

"Very well, Mr Viking," said Mr Greenbean, taking the phone, "you may interview Sydney so long as you stick to the facts. Perhaps we could meet in Cottam's Wood at three-thirty this afternoon. The scenery there is quite splendid and ideal for photographs."

The Star photographer chewed gum and his eyes lacked interest as he stood underneath the larches in Cottam's Wood. "If you ask me, this is a wild goose chase," he said grumpily, thinking to himself that he preferred to be on the terraces at the United match, rather than photographing some blooming "superbike".

"Nobody *is* asking you, boyo," said Harry Viking rather unpleasantly. "So just stick to taking pictures like you're paid to do."

The Greenbeans arrived. It was the work of mere moments to untie Cyclops and lift him from the roofrack of the car.

"You must be Sydney Greenbean," Harry Viking said. "So this is the famous bike. Danny has told me all about it."

"We thrashed them nineteen–eleven," said Sydney.

"That's quite enough of that, my lad," said Mr Greenbean crossly. "If there's anything people can't stand, it's someone who gloats when they win, and I won't have it."

Sydney could only blush, and apologise.

Soon *The Star* photographer began to chew his chewing gum more quickly than he had ever chewed gum before. Cyclops set off down a country lane all by himself, alone.

"Hey, that's some trick," said the photographer, snapping pictures and running backwards at the same time. "How's it done?"

"It's not a trick," said Sydney. "When are you going to take pictures of me?"

"Later," said Harry Viking, scribbling furiously. "What else does this bike do?"

"It's a good goalie."

"Amazing," said the reporter. He meant it. "And what exactly is it up to, now?"

They had paused, for the moment, in the shade of a large willow tree. Such trees have a habit of losing branches in a storm, and this tree had done precisely that—a branch had flattened a section of the hawthorn hedge and Cyclops was staring through the gap. A herd of cows stared back at him.

Perhaps the bicycle was curious—who knows? It is certainly true to say that Cyclops went among the cows, and set them moving.

One thing led to another. Sydney sped after his bike, calling out, "Cyclops! Here! Come back!"

Harry Viking sped after Sydney, whooping with delight. "That devil of a machine's chasing the cattle. What a scoop. Man, this is sensational! Get its *picture*!" he yelled to the photographer.

And the cows lurched about the field until their great heavy bodies were steaming with the effort of it all. *The Star* photographer, down on one muddy knee, took action shots of the wonderfully photogenic chaos.

Mr Greenbean watched these events with a sinking heart, for he knew the Press; he could tell what was likely to happen. And it did.

This is what he saw when he opened the paper a few days later:

THE STAR

MAD-DOG BIKE TERRORISES LOCAL CATTLE!

EXCLUSIVE BY STAR REPORTER, HAROLD VIKING.

"Next time I shoot to kill," warns farmer.

"I knew it!" Mr Greenbean groaned. "Our son has made the front page, Margaret. See for yourself."

Sydney, too, was disappointed as he read the paper over his mum's shoulder, but for a different reason. He was covered in mud from head to foot, as rugby players are, and not a bit like himself. "People won't know me," he complained.

"And a jolly good thing too!" said Mrs Greenbean.

By tea-time a crowd had gathered at the front of the Greenbean house in Skyline Drive. Some of these were sensation-seekers and sightseers, but it was very obvious that many were reporters from other newspapers. Mr Greenbean described them as vultures with flasks.

Mrs Greenbean said to her husband that it was amazing so many people in the world had so little to do. She went out as far as the front gate to say that neither she, nor her husband, nor her son Sydney had anything to say.

Later that evening, the Greenbeans' house appeared on the television news. The front door of 54 Skyline Drive filled the screen.

"I could open it and wave to the Nation!" thought Sydney.

The house appeared for a few seconds more, and then a man came on to talk about the weather.

And this was how it went on. The Greenbeans stayed indoors that weekend, and played Monopoly.

But of course, there is always other News. As the week wore on the Vultures faded away and (as Mr Greenbean put it rather nicely) found another carcass to pick. Sydney Greenbean was able to go to school on Wednesday, and do ordinary things like talk to Robert Foote about football, and buy jelly babies.

When Sydney came home from school on Thursday there was a white Rolls Royce at his front door. The driver wore a peaked cap and he was fast asleep at the wheel. Interesting, thought Sydney.

Mr and Mrs Greenbean were having tea in the front room with a tall, stout stranger and his daughter.

Sydney noticed that the tall, stout
stranger was one of those people who use
their saucer as an ashtray. His daughter
wore a pink fur coat with matching hat.
She seemed to be about Sydney's own age.

"Ah, Sydney," Mr Greenbean began,
"this is Mr Samuel Biggsitt and his
daughter, Olivia."

"How do you do," said Sydney, as he
had been taught.

"Mr Biggsitt would like to speak to
you."

"Why?"

"I want to talk money, boy!" boomed Samuel Biggsitt. "I want to make you an offer you can't refuse, but first take my Olivia and show her the merchandise."

Sydney looked blank. "He means your bicycle, dear," explained Mrs Greenbean. "Show Olivia your bicycle."

Cyclops was waiting for them in the middle of the garage when they got there, and Olivia Biggsitt whispered that it was very strange how he didn't just topple over.

Then she wanted to ride him. Sydney explained that Cyclops no longer behaved as an ordinary bicycle—he failed to budge a millimetre if sat upon. "But watch this," and Sydney showed off just a little, as people tend to do when they have an audience. You see, Sydney had been teaching Cyclops new tricks instead of wasting all his time watching television.

"Now sit up and beg," Sydney said—and Cyclops obliged by rearing up on his back wheel.

Olivia was obviously impressed by what she saw. "I haven't finished yet," said Sydney. They did their matador trick. Cyclops was the bull, of course, since his handlebars resembled horns, and Sydney faced him with a curtain in his hands. Olivia Biggsitt applauded generously as Sydney fooled Cyclops every time by stepping aside at the last moment.

"That's awfully clever!" she said. "Is this the only bicycle in the world who can do that?"

"I think so," Sydney said.

"Then Daddy shall want me to have him. Guess what he bought me for Christmas?"

"I give up."

"A reindeer. Do you know anyone who has a reindeer?"

"No. Only you," said Sydney. "Did your dad win his money on the lottery?"

"He doesn't do the lottery. He collects things—hotels, mainly. He's got chains of them all over the place. Shall we go?"

Sydney quite liked Olivia Biggsitt. All the same, he decided that he did not want to sell his bicycle to her because he'd grown quite fond of Cyclops and enjoyed teaching him things.

Mr Biggsitt had his cheque-book on his
knee when they got back. "Okay boy,
let's talk business. How much will you
take for this bicycle?"

"Well, I've never thought about selling
Cyclops, Sir," Sydney said, "and I'd
rather keep him if you don't mind. He
plays on my football team. We are the
Greenbeans."

"Football, eh? How's about ten
thousand pounds? Think about that. Ten
thousand pounds is some transfer fee.
Take it or leave it."

"I'll take it," said Sydney.

Now that the deal was done, the chauffeur was roused from his sleep and obliged to put Cyclops into the back of the white Rolls Royce. Sydney felt quite sad as he watched the Biggsitts drive away, but he was comforted by the thought of what he could buy with the cheque in his hand.

"First I'll buy a new bike, and its name will be Ziggy," he said to his mum and dad, "and then I'll buy jelly babies for my whole class in school, and some jeans. Then I'll buy football kits for the Greenbeans so that we all look the same."

"You will do no such thing, my lad," Mrs Greenbean said. "That money will go straight into the bank for a rainy day."

Robert Foote, Sydney, and some other members of the Greenbean Football Team walked home from school the next day. They had arranged for a session of shooting practice in the park, because in recent games they had not been putting away their goal-scoring chances as they should.

Some of the team were not happy that their goalie had been sold.

"You might have waited, Sydney," said Agnes Hillock, "until Fergy's chicken-pox went away."

"I know," said Sydney. "I was selfish, I see that now. But it's too late."

"How much did you get for Cyclops?"

"Quite a lot," Sydney said. His mother had warned him not to tell the whole street his business.

The team paused to look at an eye-catching poster. It said:

"I've never been to a circus," said Robert Foote.

"Neither have I," said Agnes Hillock. Victoria Blower wondered whether the circus would have elephants, tigers and a lion-tamer. Then the Greenbeans went home to change.

There was a note waiting for Sydney when he got in.

Sydney
I have gone to the bank.
Look in the garage and you
will see why. That stupid
bike – I could wring its neck!

Cyclops had come home!

To judge by the state of him, he'd come a long way, for his lower parts glistened with thick, moist mud. Sydney thought it likely that he'd travelled throughout the night to be here.

"You are some bike, Cyclops," he said, patting him fondly on the seat. "I guess the Biggsitts want their transfer fee back. Too bad. Let's play football."

If Sydney Greenbean thought that having a bicycle like Cyclops would always be marvellous fun, and that there would never be any problems, then he was as wrong as could be. There were lots of problems. For example, Cyclops escaped one day when Mrs Greenbean went out to switch on the central heating. Two policemen brought him back, and they were not smiling.

"Oh dear!" Mrs Greenbean gasped
when she saw them at her door. No one
likes to see policemen at their door.

"We found this prowling around the
circus tent without good reason, my good
lady. Didn't we, Joe?"

"That is correct," said Joe.

"On apprehending it, we discovered a
name and address on a little metal plate. I
trust it belongs to you?"

"Yes! Well … I … Oh dear. It's my
son's actually."

"Does this bicycle know its Green Cross Code, ma'am?"

"I don't think he does, Constable."

"Then he's a danger to other road-users, isn't he?"

"A considerable danger," added Joe.

Mrs Greenbean realised that this was so, and promised to put a chain round Cyclops' back wheel so that he couldn't wander again.

Later, at tea, Mrs Greenbean told her family all that had happened, and she was careful to describe her thoughts and feelings when she saw two uniformed policemen at her door.

"And, Sydney Greenbean," she finished at last, "if there is any more trouble from that nuisance of a bicycle, it will have to go!"

Once every three weeks, Mr and Mrs Greenbean had their windows cleaned, upstairs and down, by a window cleaner.

It was a Friday afternoon. Mr Greenbean had come home early from the office and was now nicely settled in the kitchen with a welcome cup of tea. Sydney was there too, writing a Get Well Soon card to Fergy, whose chicken-pox hadn't cleared up yet. Mrs Greenbean hunted through her purse for money to pay the window cleaner. All of a sudden, the window cleaner himself burst through the back door without so much as a knock.

There was a wild look in the man's eye. And now that he was here, he seemed uncertain whether to fasten his mad gaze on Mrs Greenbean, on Mr Greenbean, or on Sydney.

"That bike followed me up my ladder."

"I beg your pardon?" said Mrs Greenbean as the man poked a finger upwards.

"It's up there. On the roof. It followed me up. I must be crazy, mustn't I? Yes. Pigs will fly, next!" And he wiped his forehead with a dirty, damp rag.

"Calm down, my man," said Mr Greenbean, as Mrs Greenbean boiled up the kettle again. She believed that tea cured most things.

Sydney went outside to see for himself what this was all about, and found that he was not alone—the whole street had come out to stare up at Cyclops.

The Greenbeans lived in a block of six
terraced houses. Cyclops was travelling
along the crest of the roof with an easy
and even graceful movement. It was as if,
said one member of the excited crowd,
they were gazing at a bicycle ridden by a
phantom. When Cyclops came to a
chimney, he simply shimmied round it.

It was marvellous—and there was
more! Between one block of houses and
the next there was a gap, and Cyclops
crossed this gap on a single telephone
wire, high above the heads of everyone.

"Oooo," sighed the crowd, amazed.

"I say, that's young Greenbean's bike up there, isn't it?"

"How on earth does it do these things? Remote control, or what?"

"By jove, look. It's got itself tangled up in Harry Gurkin's TV aerial. *He* won't like that, if I know Harry Gurkin."

Harry Gurkin himself appeared in his braces and slippers. He addressed his remarks to Mr Greenbean, and as he spoke, his tattooed arms thrashed the air like windmills. "That thing has ruined my picture. And I was watching snooker. Well, I just want you to know that I've phoned for the fire-brigade, mate."

In no way was this an idle threat, for the fire-brigade turned into the crowded street a minute or two later.

People applauded the helmeted men who now sprang into action. They applauded the turn-table ladder as it reached for the sky. They applauded and they cheered the tiny figure who scaled the long ladder and carried Cyclops to safety across his shoulder. Most people who were present that day, including Sydney Greenbean, felt that firemen were wonderful and deserved every penny of their pay.

Later that day, Sydney's parents talked to him quietly and seriously about his bicycle's future.

"The thing is," said Mr Greenbean, "we simply cannot go on like this any longer. Matters are getting out of hand. Our neighbours will turn against us, Sydney, if there are further incidents like the one today. You heard what Harry Gurkin had to say."

"Horrible man," said Mrs Greenbean.

"I agree—but even horrible people have their rights, Margaret. Cyclops will have to go."

"What will we do with him?" Sydney asked.

"We will give him one absolutely final chance," said Mr Greenbean, "and if all else fails, we shall offer him to the County Museum."

Seven people with seven bicycles gathered in Robert Foote's garage. There wasn't much room to move in there without stepping on a neat little pile of nuts and bolts. Many mudguards, many saddles, and many other bits of bikes littered the floor, giving the impression that a big metal jigsaw was under construction.

The entire Greenbean Football Team was hard at work, with the exceptions of Fergy and Rex. One of these was sick and the other was at the circus.

"Spanner, please," said Agnes Hillock. Ivan Gumsworthy passed her a spanner and Agnes removed the saddle of her bike. She passed the spanner to Victoria Blower, who accepted it with oily fingers. The back wheel of Wally Winters' bike hit the floor with a clatter.

Sydney, meanwhile, had just finished

taking Cyclops to pieces, and it has to be said that the poor bike looked fit only for the scrap-heap without its wheels, mudguards, handlebars and chain.

Robert Foote supervised the whole operation, since this was his idea. It was the kind of idea that appeals only to those who are desperate. Briefly, the idea was this: Cyclops would cease to exist as a separate and independent bicycle with his own identity. Bits of him would be removed, and swopped around with bits taken from other bicycles. At the end of the day, Sydney would still have a bike to call his own, but one that would no longer cause aggravation to his family or the local community.

It was a bold idea and it deserved to work. But would it?

"Okay," Sydney said at last, "that's it. I'll walk about the garage and see if it follows me."

By "it" he meant the reconstituted bicycle. Cyclops, or rather, what used to be Cyclops, now had Agnes Hillock's saddle; Robert Foote's front wheel; Wally Winters' rear wheel; Victoria Blower's handlebars; Ivan Gumsworthy's mudguards; and Samuel Turtle's chain.

The new bike lay on the ground without so much as a twitch. "Looks good," said Wally Winters.

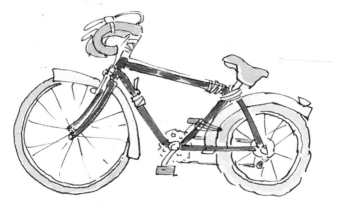

"All the same," said Sydney, "I shall try our matador trick, to be sure. Here, Torro! Charge!" Cyclops—what remained of him—failed to charge. It seemed that in a curious way, Cyclops was gone.

At suppertime, Mr Greenbean said how happy he was to hear that Robert's idea had proved successful. "Neat trick, that. Imaginative. It would be very handy if that technique worked on human beings. I can think of one or two people …"

The phone interrupted his thoughts at that moment, and as he listened to what was being said by the person at the other end of the line, Mr Greenbean's eyebrows gathered into a frown above his spectacles. He replaced the receiver with a neat click.

"What is it, Wilfred?" asked Mrs Greenbean.

"Well you may ask, my dear. That was Victoria Blower's father. He says that young Vicky's bicycle has disappeared."

"Stolen?" said Mrs Greenbean. "Or ...?"

"Exactly. And what is more, Samuel Turtle's bike has vanished too. I must say that I am beginning to suspect the worst. Go and look, Sydney."

Sydney went, looked, saw, and came back again. "Bike's gone," he said.

Grave looks were exchanged by Mr and Mrs Greenbean. Clearly, these developments could not be taken lightly.

At this same moment, but in a different place, two policemen on patrol duty parked their car under a street lamp near the children's playground. They ate a hamburger roll together, and drank coffee from a flask as a passing shower of rain beat lightly on the windscreen of their car.

As they sat there quietly chewing, and thinking their own thoughts, strange noises fell upon their ears.

"There's somebody over there in the park, Mike," said Joe.

"Funny, that," said Mike, "all the kids are in bed."

"Or at the circus," said Joe.

The noises seemed to grow louder— metallic clinks and clanks and rattles.

"I wonder, could someone be trying to steal a swing or a roundabout, Joe?" Mike said thoughtfully.

45

"You and I are familiar with human nature, Mike," said Joe, "and we know that some people will steal anything. I think we should look into this. Bring your torch."

They left their car and crept towards the park like shadows in the night. And strangely enough, they saw seven bicycles in the public park, playing follow-my-leader up the slide and down the slide, and all by the light of the moon.

"Well, strike me pink," Joe whispered behind a bush. "That sort of carry-on can't be legal, can it?"

"I'll question them," said Mike, stepping out from the bush.

He said, "Stop in the name of the law," but it was no use. The first bicycle jolly nearly ran right over him, causing him to jump sideways into a bed of freshly planted pansies.

"Come back here for questioning!" called Mike—quite uselessly, for the offender disappeared into the night with the other bicycles in tow.

"Right! Radio for help," cried Mike.

"We will certainly get the blighters for resisting arrest!" said Joe.

Some time later that evening. Mr Greenbean learned something of these events by telephone. It was very noticeable how the frown above his spectacles deepened the more he listened, and how there was a strain in his voice as he said, "Yes. Yes, of course, Inspector. I will come down to the station at once."

"Wilfred—what is it?"

"I hardly know how to tell you, my dear. I'm afraid it's Cyclops."

"What about him?" said Sydney, speaking from the top of the stairs in his pyjamas.

"They've been arrested. All of them. It seems they were disturbing the peace and the police have put them in jail."

It did not take all the King's horses and all the King's men to put Cyclops the bicycle together again—the Greenbeans took just twenty minutes flat once the bikes got out of jail the following morning.

Sydney Greenbean had to accept that his bicycle was in total disgrace. Parents warned their children to keep their bikes away from Cyclops at all costs. He was a bad influence and a ringleader of the worst kind, they said. The very existence of The Greenbean Football Team was put in jeopardy.

One of those parents, Mrs Gumsworthy, let Mrs Greenbean know just how she felt by saying "Hello," in the supermarket. Nothing else—just that sharp "Hello!" from a woman who normally talked the leg off a stool.

"I was cut to the bone, Wilfred," Mrs Greenbean confided afterwards.

"I shall take him to the County Museum at once," said Mr Greenbean, putting on his overcoat. Sydney had to go too. Cyclops refused to follow Mr Greenbean.

The curator at the County Museum listened carefully to what they had to say, even though it was almost closing time. "Your bicycle may be 'la crème de la crème', Sir," he said, partly in French, "but where would we put it? We have no room. Space is a question of the utmost importance. Do you expect us to throw out our prehistoric Great Elk and exhibit in its place a bicycle from the late twentieth century?"

He spoke with his hand resting fondly on the shin bone of the magnificent beast, which was clearly one of his favourite specimens.

"You mean you don't want him?" said Sydney.

"It is out of the question," the curator said.

The Greenbeans came home again. Mr Greenbean said to his wife that the curator of the County Museum was an impossible man.

"But nothing has changed. This simply means that something more drastic is called for. Cyclops will have to go!"

51

Sydney and Robert walked to Cottam's Bridge. Sadly, Cyclops' last day had come. They intended to lower him from the bridge to the water below, suspended from a rope, and then let him fall gently into the soft mud of the river-bed.

"He was some goalie," Sydney said to his friend as he made fast the rope.

"He certainly was," said Robert. "He was a better goalie than Fergy."

Cyclops swayed to and fro on the way down. As soon as the water swallowed Cyclops, Sydney let go of the rope without watching him sink.

Like most people in life who have made a tough decision, he wondered for some time whether he had done the right thing. Then he remembered how Mrs Gumsworthy had been rude to his mother in the supermarket because of Cyclops.

And besides, Fergy was getting jealous.
He'd written a letter to Sydney, asking was
it true that nobody wanted him to be the
Greenbean goalie any more. Friends,
thought Sydney, are more important than
bicycles.

"It was the only way," he said to Robert.

"It was," agreed Robert.

At half-past seven that evening. Mr
Greenbean went out to the dustbin, and
there was Cyclops standing in the back
garden. Mr Greenbean could not have been
more surprised if he'd seen a ghost.
"Margaret," he said, "*Margaret*. Come
into the garden this minute!"

"For goodness sake, Wilfred, what is
the ...?"

Mrs Greenbean did not finish her sentence; she saw with her own eyes what the matter was.

It was very noticeable how strands of river-weeds trailed from Cyclops' spokes, like ribbons. Sydney began to pick these off, one by one.

This was beyond a joke, Mr Greenbean said. He now gave full vent to one of his few fits of fury. "You … you … silly, stupid bike! What do we have to do, eh? Don't tell me. I know. We have to bury one blasted wheel in Scotland, and one blasted wheel in Wales, and the rest of you in the Isle of Wight! Right?"

"Wilfred, *please*," said Mrs Greenbean.

"Well, what do you expect? Why does it pick on us? Look—no rope! Can it swim? Its name is Houdini! I'll tell you where that thing should be—down the road."

"What do you mean, Wilfred?"

"I mean it belongs in the blasted CIRCUS!"

Sydney Greenbean was easy to spot in the queue of people waiting to get into the circus—he was the only one with a bike.

He and Robert Foote chewed jelly babies as they read the large sign over the flap of the tent:

ODDFELLOW'S MAGICAL BIG TOP CIRCUS SHOW

INTERNATIONAL ARTISTES   CLOWNS   JUNGLE BEASTS

Sydney gave his money to the ticket-man, who wore an ancient top hat and a suit with tails. The folded whip on the table suggested that as well as the ticket-man, he might also be the Ringmaster.

Which he was. And the lion-tamer. This was Norbert Oddfellow the Third, owner of The Oddfellow Big Top Circus.

"Do I have to pay for my bike too, or can he come in free?" asked Sydney.

"Depends. Bikes are free on Fridays."

"This *is* a Friday, Sir."

"Then you're a lucky son-of-a-gun. Next please!"

The circus ring was a patch of flattened grass, surrounded by a circle of curved, coloured blocks.

"There should be sawdust, you know," whispered Robert as he and Sydney settled themselves in the front row. "My dad says there's always sawdust in a circus ring."

"Dads are sometimes wrong about things," said Sydney.

Robert Foote expected to see a band, too—but this show didn't have one. However, the Ringmaster did play some trumpet music on an old wind-up gramophone. This was the signal for the fun to begin!

First the trapeze artiste came on. She did her act on a bar that was only a little higher than a farm gate. Her hair, as she swung to and fro in her spangled costume, trailed through the grass, and some people in the audience were rude to her.

"Hey, where's your safety net?"

"Mind you don't fall and hurt yourself."

But then the people sat up as they wheeled in THE KING OF THE JUNGLE (these were the words on the side of the cage). This was a great, shaggy beast, very faded and very old. A voice behind Sydney said that it had false teeth. The Ringmaster prodded him through the bars of the cage, but failed to rouse him from a deep sleep.

"Is that a lion or a hearthrug?" someone shouted.

When the king of the jungle had come and gone, the Ringmaster changed the record on the gramophone and cracked his whip three times, very loudly.

"Elephant music!" said Robert, as clowns ran out with drum-shaped stools. "The elephants put their feet up on those."

Six black and white cows came through a flap in the tent and plodded round the ring. When one of these cows lowered its head to munch grass, it received a flick from the Ringmaster's whip. Two of the cows stopped, raised a front leg, and placed a hoof delicately on a drum.

Robert Foote was not happy. "This isn't much of a circus," he mumbled.

The people in the row behind Sydney laughed so much that they slid out of their seats. Other members of the audience hooted loudly, and there were wild cries of "Moooooo" and "Free milk!"

"Booo! Call yourself a circus?"

"Bring on the sheep," called the crowd. "We want sheep!"

Now this kind of hooligan behaviour was very hard to bear for the poor old Ringmaster, who sank into a chair with his head in his hands.

Norbert Oddfellow the Third knew that they wanted elephants. But where would he get elephants in this day and age? Besides, it was *harder* to train cows than elephants, but the public didn't understand these things. They were vulgar, and ignorant, and life was mighty tough.

"Excuse me, Sir," said a voice, "I think I can help." It was a boy and his bike.

"Get away, boy, I'm finished. There is no help. They don't want cows; they want elephants. They don't even want elephants; what they want is television.

The Circus is doomed. A chapter in the history of mankind ends here tonight."

But Sydney Greenbean had something to say, and he made a point of saying it. And Norbert Oddfellow, when he had listened, shouted, "Pickle my brains, boy, I'll take a chance on you. I will!" He rushed back into the ring. "*Ladies and gentlemen*. Take your seats, please, I thank you one and all. Oddfellow's Big Top Circus Show is proud to present to you tonight *Mr Sydney Greenbean* and his *Performing Bicycle*."

Just to get the act started, Sydney got Cyclops to sit and beg—but Cyclops seemed very much at home and soon tired of such tame stuff. He zoomed twice round the ring—once on his back wheel and once on his front wheel—and followed that with a series of cartwheels across the grass that brought the astonished audience to their feet. Even Sydney was amazed. Cyclops was a natural showman. Sydney called for hoops. Cyclops jumped through them.

When the applause died down the Ringmaster changed the mood by changing records. A barrel rolled into the centre of the ring and out climbed a very short clown. He took Cyclops by the handlebars, and did a slow dance around the ring to the sound of a scratchy waltz. It was sheer magic!

The audience could not help themselves, they clapped in three–four time, and sang the Blue Danube between their laughter and their smiles, and the tears rolling down Norbert's face saturated the Oddfellow's snowy-white beard. "Ah," he sighed, "beautiful! Who needs elephants?"

Soon it was over, and all that was left of the crowd was its rubbish. It was difficult, though, to calm down Mr Oddfellow, for he was a happy man, and happiness made him want to talk and talk. "What an artist you have there, my young friend Greenbean! Mysterious, incredible, inexplicable. He is like the Circus, my boy, do you know that? He is a metaphor for life itself!"

Sydney made no reply to this, for he didn't understand a word of it.

"I have to go now," he said. "Take care of my bicycle, please, Mr Oddfellow. His name is Cyclops."

"Thank you, Sydney Greenbean," said Norbert Oddfellow, "very much indeed."

Sydney went home alone. Mr and Mrs Greenbean said they were very proud of him for ending their problem with such a wonderful idea. After three mugs of cocoa, the Greenbeans went to bed.

For a few months afterwards Sydney glanced over his shoulder at odd moments, half expecting to see Cyclops following behind him. But he never did.